The Tale of the Pronghorned Cantaloupe

Copyright © 2010, Story by Sabra Brown Steinsiek
Translation & Illustrations by Noël Chilton

Published by Rio Grande Books
925 Salamanca NW
Los Ranchos, NM 87107-5647
505-344-9382
www.nmsantos.com

Printed in the United States of America
Book Design: Paul Rhetts

All rights reserved. No part of this book may be reproduced or transmitted in
any form by any means without permission in writing from the publisher.

Library of Congress Cataloging-in-Publication Data

Steinsiek, Sabra Brown.
  The tale of the pronghorned cantaloupe/ by Sabra Brown Steinsiek ; translation
[into Spanish] and illustrations by Noel Chilton.
        p. cm.
  Summary: Relates the adventures of a young boy and his fearless daschund in the
days when the wild pronghorned cantaloupe roamed New Mexico.

  ISBN 978-1-890689-85-8 (pbk. : alk. paper)

  [1. Muskmelon–Fiction. 2. Dachshunds–Fiction. 3. Dogs–Fiction. 4. Humorous sto-
ries. 5. Spanish language materials–Bilingual.] I. Chilton, Noel, ill. II. Title.
  PZ73S7563 2009
  [E]–dc22
                                                2009034486

Dedications

Dedicated to the memory of my dad, James Herbert Brown, who really did walk in all that snow and consider the worth of a snake compared with keeping his mother. Love you Dad!—Sabra Brown Steinsiek

For Mom and Dad who always keep the light on for me.—Noël Chilton

My daddy grew up on a farm in New Mexico. He said it was a rough area, where not much grew except snow and snakes.

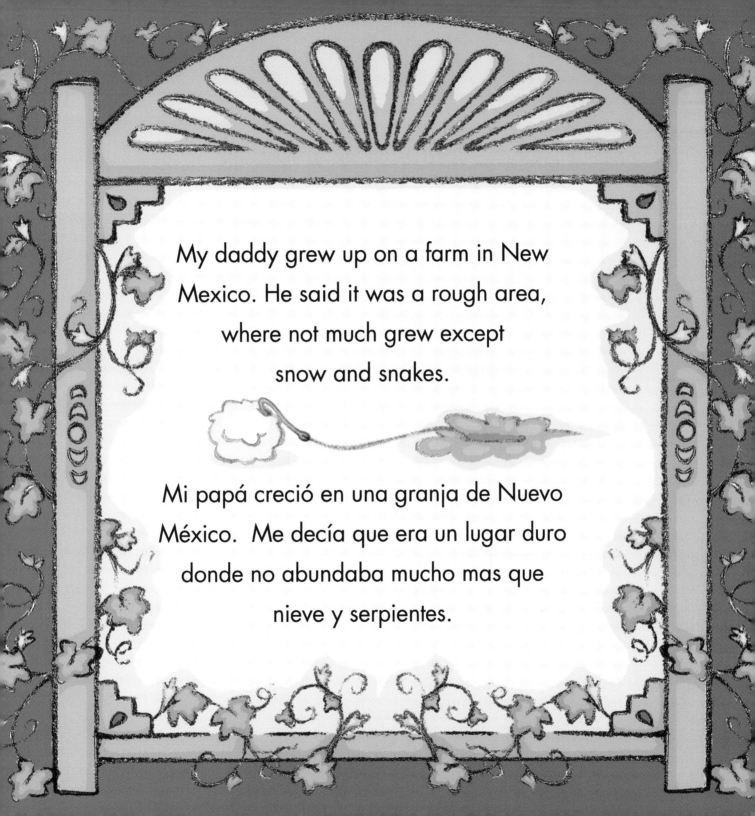

Mi papá creció en una granja de Nuevo México. Me decía que era un lugar duro donde no abundaba mucho mas que nieve y serpientes.

He often told me about walking to school, and the funny thing was, every time he told it the road would be longer and the snow deeper than the time before!

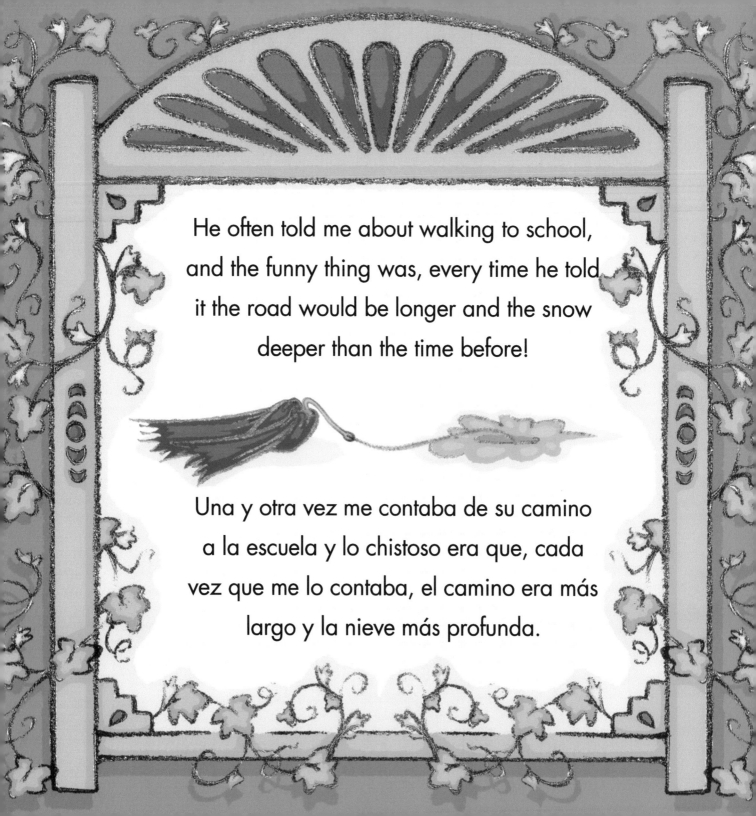

Una y otra vez me contaba de su camino a la escuela y lo chistoso era que, cada vez que me lo contaba, el camino era más largo y la nieve más profunda.

He also told me about the time he brought a
snake home and his mother told him he had
to choose her or the snake . . . but
that's a story for another day.

Además, me dijo del día que llevó una
serpiente a casa y su mamá le dijo que tenía
que escoger entre ella y la serpiente...pero
esa es una historia para otro día.

My favorite of his stories was about the
fall roundup of the wild pronghorn cantaloupe. Now
these looked a lot like the cantaloupes you see at the
grocery store, except that they had sharp double-pronged
horns growing out where the stem would be and...

Mi cuento favorito fué la de la cosecha de los melones
cornudos de otoño. Esos melones se parecían mucho a
los melones que compras en el mercado, excepto que
tenían cuernos con dos puntas filosas que salían de
donde se conectaría el rabo y...

…rolled across the plains in herds. They would use those horns to steer with, dipping down on one side or the other, depending on the direction they wanted to go.

…rodaban en grupos por todas las llanuras. Ocupaban los cuernos para dirigirse, inclinandose de un lado u otro, dependiendo de a donde querían ir.

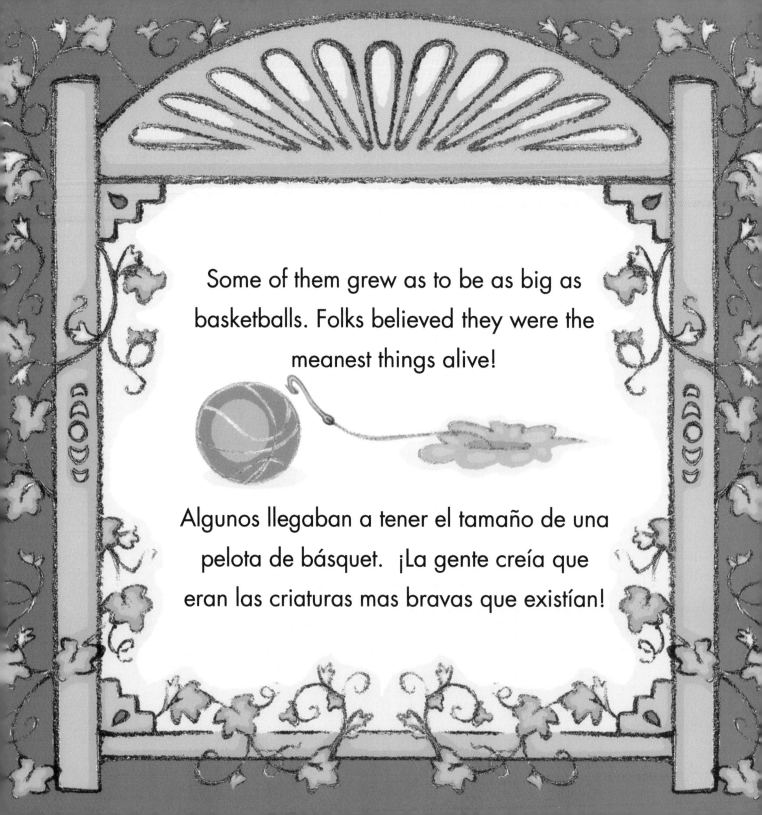

Some of them grew as to be as big as basketballs. Folks believed they were the meanest things alive!

Algunos llegaban a tener el tamaño de una pelota de básquet. ¡La gente creía que eran las criaturas mas bravas que existían!

Dad's best friend was his dog, Andy. Even though Andy was a dachshund, that dog fancied himself to be a great hunting dog, fearless and invincible.

El mejor amigo de papá fue su perro, Andy. Aunque Andy fuera perro salchicha, se creía un gran perro de casería, sin miedo e invencible.

The two of them were always together, except when Dad had to go to school.

Los dos estaban siempre juntos, menos cuando papá tenía que ir a la escuela.

Andy would wait for him on the
front porch, dreaming big dreams
for such a little dog.

Andy lo esperaba en el portal,
teniendo sueños grandes siendo
un perro tan chiquito.

Dad told me about one time when they were out hunting rabbits and Andy stumbled on a nest of the pronghorns. Those cantaloupes rolled around that dog and, just out of pure meanness, began to close in on him with those wicked horns sharp and ready to rip.

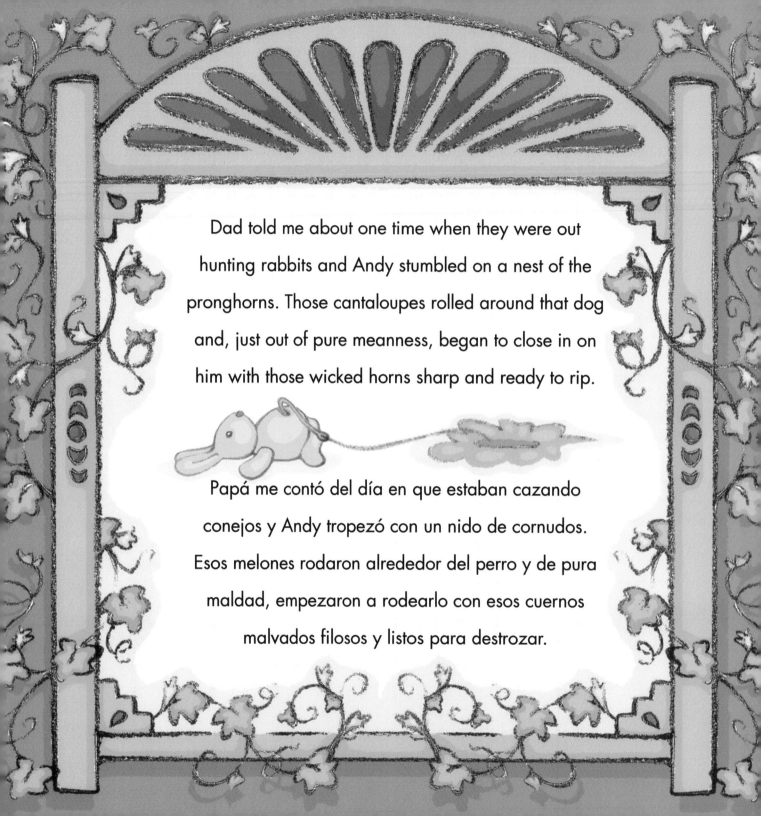

Papá me contó del día en que estaban cazando conejos y Andy tropezó con un nido de cornudos. Esos melones rodaron alrededor del perro y de pura maldad, empezaron a rodearlo con esos cuernos malvados filosos y listos para destrozar.

The sound they made was just like
the thump you hear when you tap a
cantaloupe at the grocery store today.

Hacían un ruido como el "tum"
que escuchas cuando hoy en día le das
un golpecito a un melón en el mercado.

That day there were so many of them
that they sounded like thunder as they
rolled all around Andy.

Ese día había tantos de ellos, que
sonaban como truenos en el cielo
al mismo tiempo que rodeaban a Andy.

That dog would have been a goner if Dad hadn't had his skinning knife with him. He threw it and hit one of the cantaloupes dead center, splitting it right in two! The rest of those cantaloupes scattered.

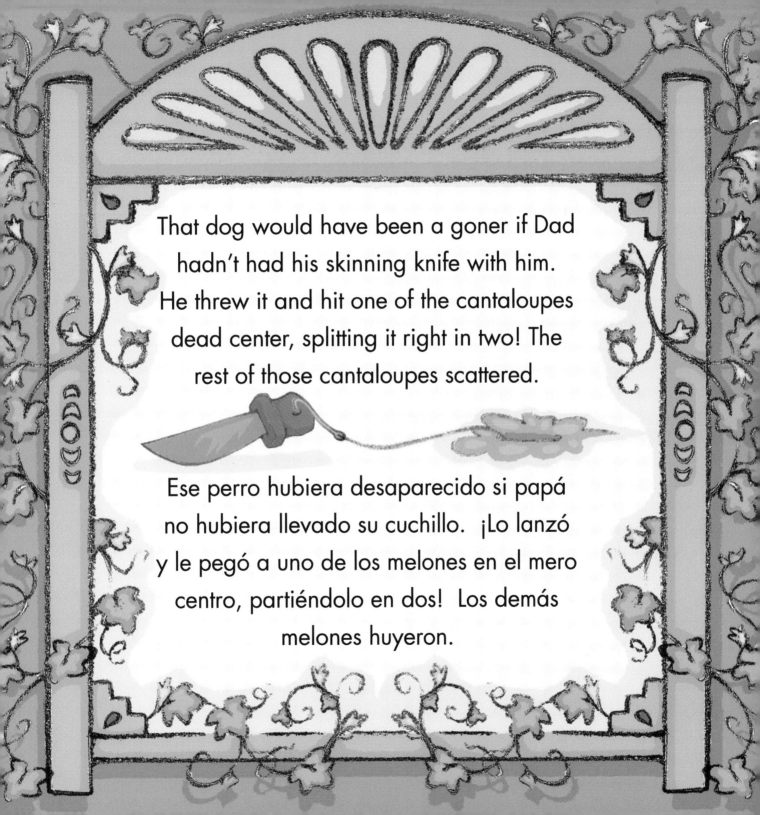

Ese perro hubiera desaparecido si papá no hubiera llevado su cuchillo. ¡Lo lanzó y le pegó a uno de los melones en el mero centro, partiéndolo en dos! Los demás melones huyeron.

Dad sat down and broke off those pronghorn antlers and used them to scoop out the sweet cantaloupe meat. They were wild and dangerous but they were good eating when you could catch one.

Papá se sentó, arrancó los cuernos, y los ocupó para sacar la carne dulce del melón. Eran salvajes y peligrosos pero sabrosos si lograbas cazar uno.

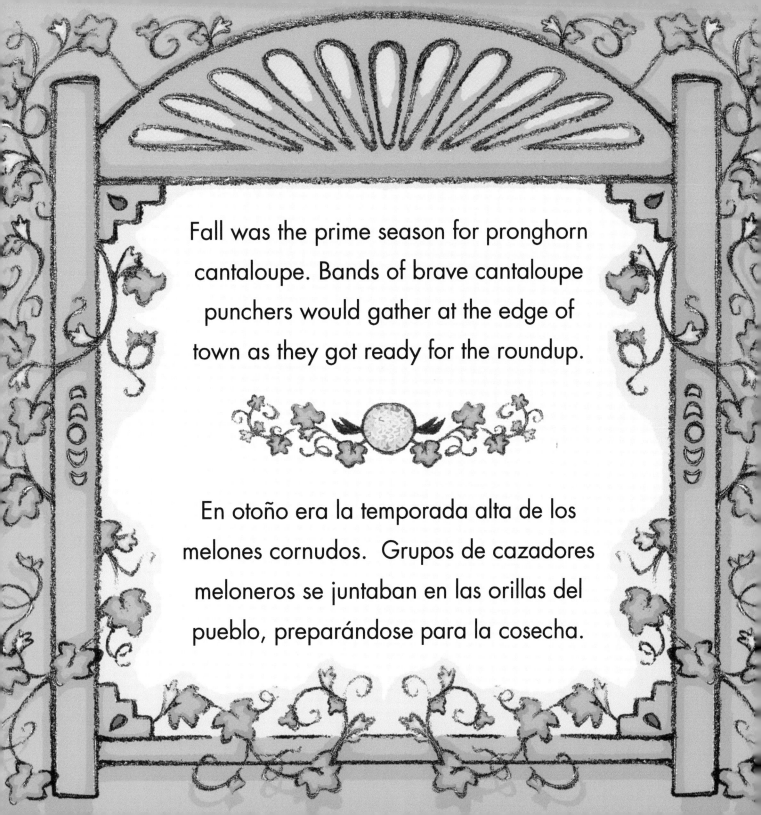

Fall was the prime season for pronghorn cantaloupe. Bands of brave cantaloupe punchers would gather at the edge of town as they got ready for the roundup.

En otoño era la temporada alta de los melones cornudos. Grupos de cazadores meloneros se juntaban en las orillas del pueblo, preparándose para la cosecha.

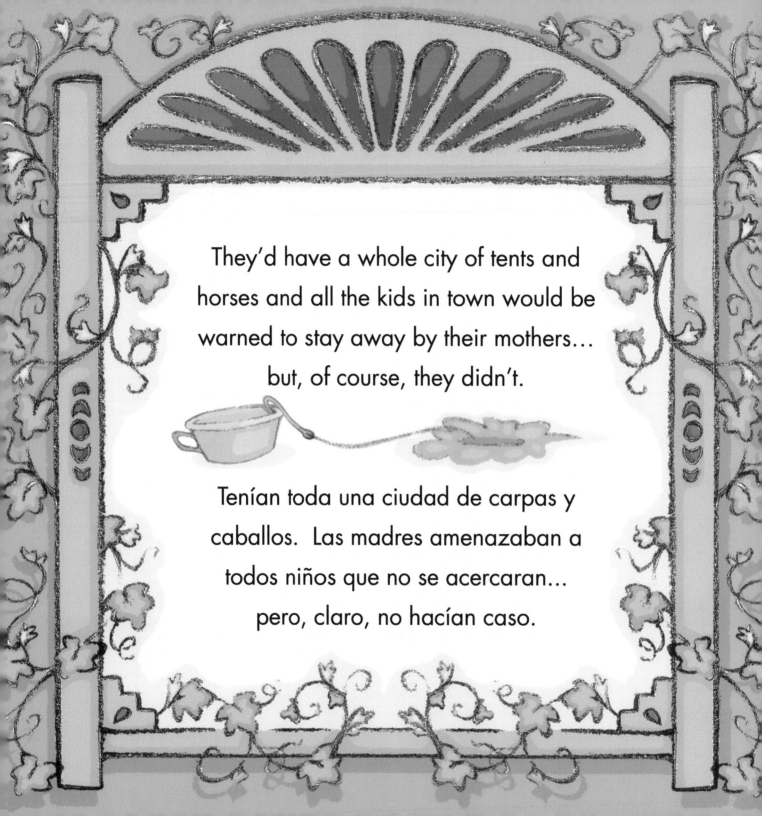

They'd have a whole city of tents and
horses and all the kids in town would be
warned to stay away by their mothers…
but, of course, they didn't.

Tenían toda una ciudad de carpas y
caballos. Las madres amenazaban a
todos niños que no se acercaran…
pero, claro, no hacían caso.

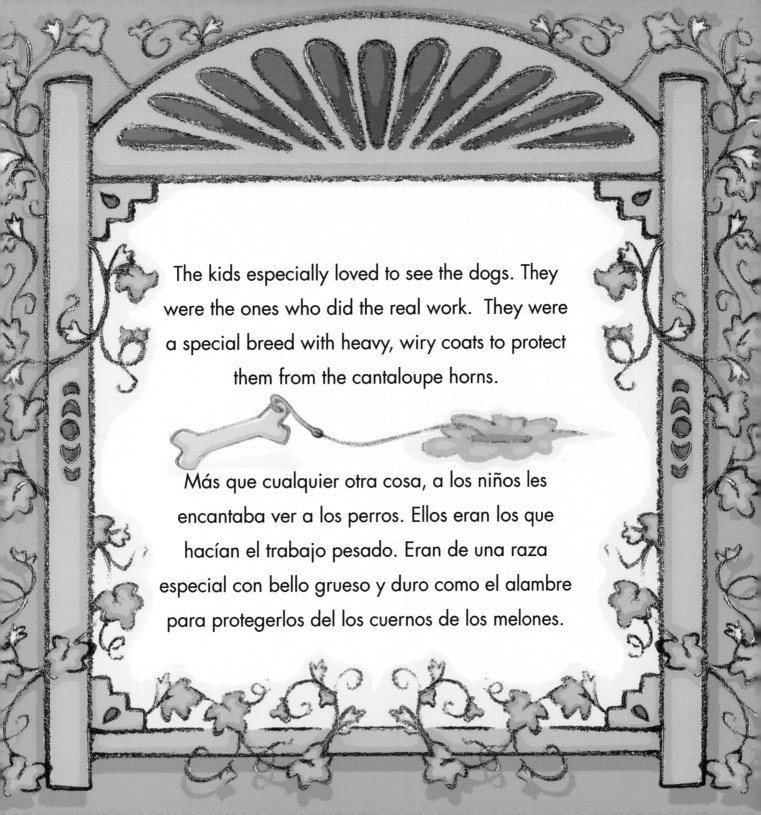

The kids especially loved to see the dogs. They were the ones who did the real work. They were a special breed with heavy, wiry coats to protect them from the cantaloupe horns.

Más que cualquier otra cosa, a los niños les encantaba ver a los perros. Ellos eran los que hacían el trabajo pesado. Eran de una raza especial con bello grueso y duro como el alambre para protegerlos del los cuernos de los melones.

And they were totally fearless, nipping at the cantaloupes to get them rolling to market. Dad said there was no finer sight than a group of melon collies setting out on the cantaloupe drive each fall.

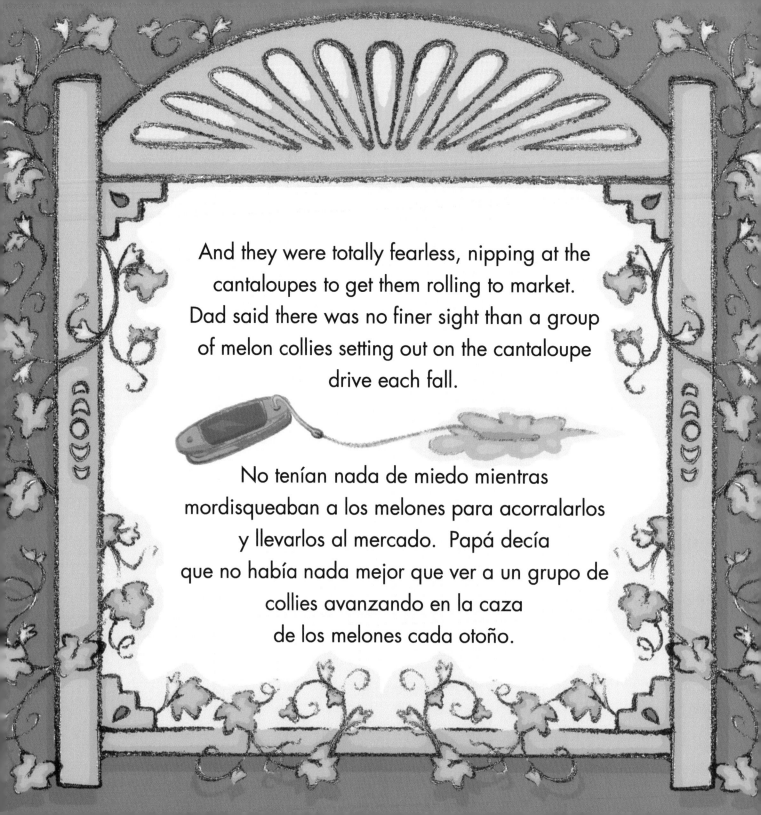

No tenían nada de miedo mientras mordisqueaban a los melones para acorralarlos y llevarlos al mercado. Papá decía que no había nada mejor que ver a un grupo de collies avanzando en la caza de los melones cada otoño.

One year there was a drought. No rain.
No snow. It was so bad that my Dad had
to go to school without complaining about
the snow, because there wasn't any!

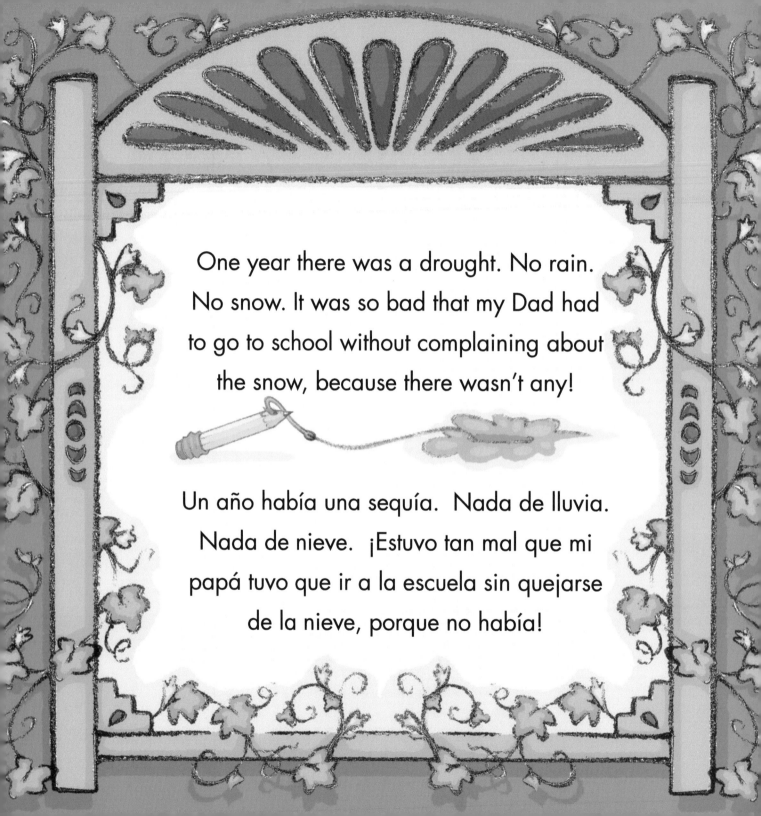

Un año había una sequía. Nada de lluvia.
Nada de nieve. ¡Estuvo tan mal que mi
papá tuvo que ir a la escuela sin quejarse
de la nieve, porque no había!

The drought continued into the next year,
and on into the one after that. Dad said
he nearly forgot what the snow looked like.
As for the snakes, they had slithered away to
someplace more pleasant.

La sequía siguió el siguiente año y el siguiente.
Papá decía que casi olvidaba como se veía
la nieve. Y por lo de las serpientes- se habían
deslizado a otro lado mas agradable.

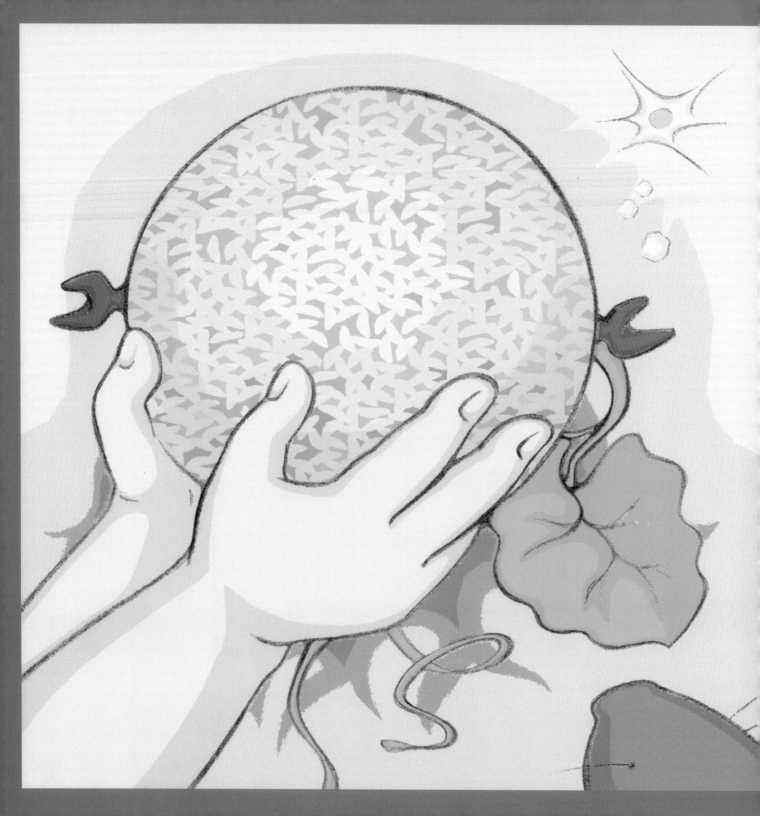

And the pronghorn cantaloupes?
Well, they were few and far between.
At the roundups, most only had stubby little
horns if they had any at all.
They had no fight in them.

Y los melones cornudos? Pues, había muy
poquitos. En las cosechas, la mayoría
tenía cuernitos cortitos si es que los tenían.
Lo bravo, se les quitó.

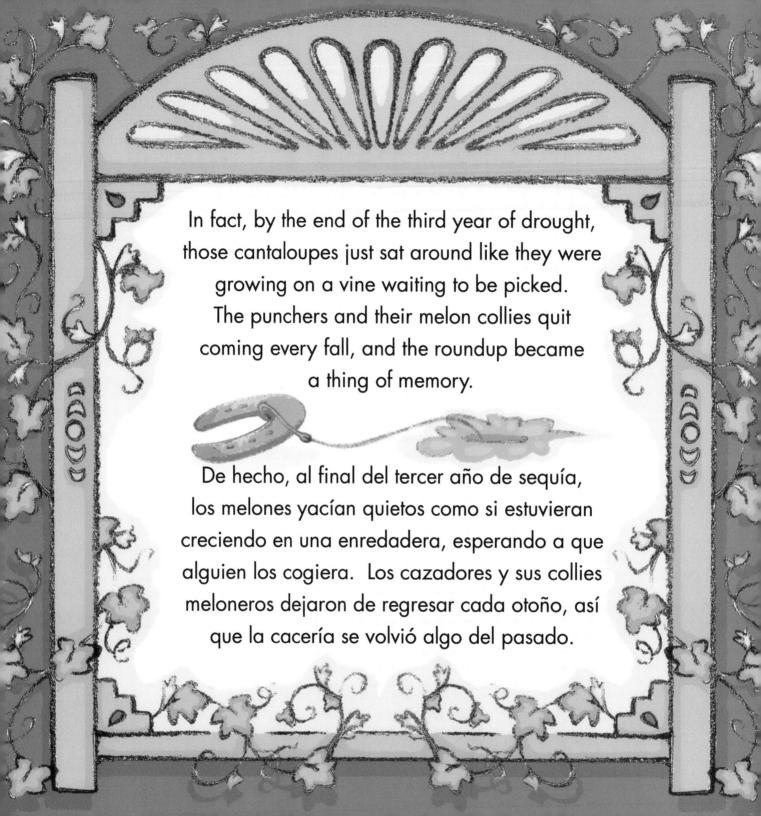

In fact, by the end of the third year of drought, those cantaloupes just sat around like they were growing on a vine waiting to be picked. The punchers and their melon collies quit coming every fall, and the roundup became a thing of memory.

De hecho, al final del tercer año de sequía, los melones yacían quietos como si estuvieran creciendo en una enredadera, esperando a que alguien los cogiera. Los cazadores y sus collies meloneros dejaron de regresar cada otoño, así que la cacería se volvió algo del pasado.

"It was a rare sight," my daddy said, "a rare sight indeed." And I never saw him eat a cantaloupe without poking it first with his knife. I don't think he ever gave up hoping that those wonderful days of the pronghorn cantaloupe would return.

"Fue algo único," decía mi papá, "algo verdaderamente único." Aun así, nunca vi a mi papá comer un melón sin primero picarlo con su cuchillo. Creo que nunca abandonó la esperanza de que volvieran esos días fantásticos de los melones cornudos.

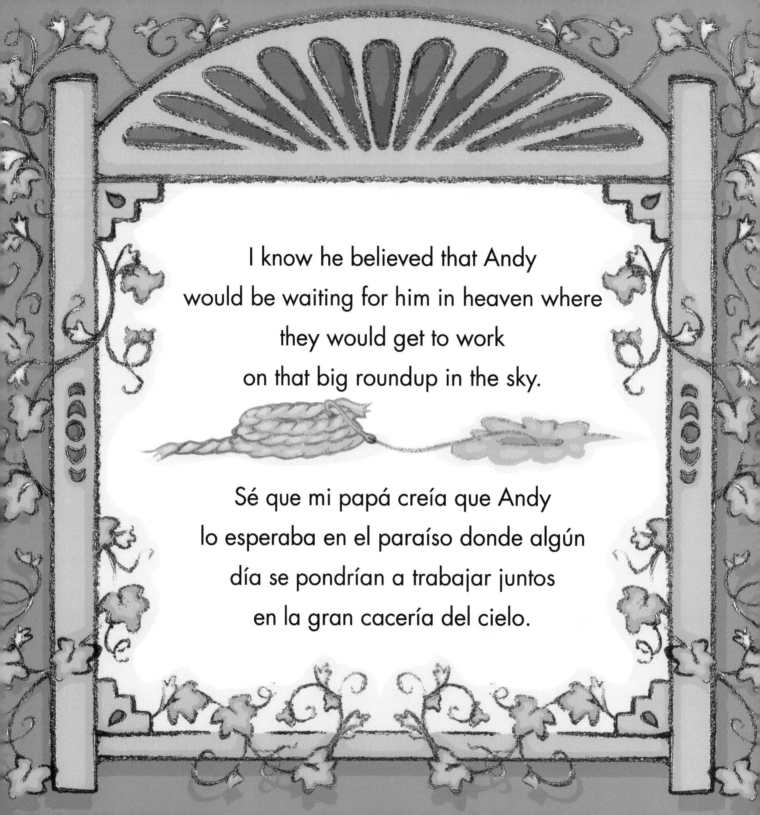

I know he believed that Andy
would be waiting for him in heaven where
they would get to work
on that big roundup in the sky.

Sé que mi papá creía que Andy
lo esperaba en el paraíso donde algún
día se pondrían a trabajar juntos
en la gran cacería del cielo.

Author

Sabra Brown Steinsiek is a life-long librarian turned author. She has written award winning romance novels for adults and a book of haiku poetry. *The Tale of the Pronghorned Cantaloupe* is her first children's book. She lives in Albuquerque with her husband and son, two cats, an insatiable curiosity, and an overactive imagination.

Illustrator

Noel Chilton migrates with the butterflies between the American Southwest and Southern Mexico. She never flies without her two boys and her colored pencil set. Both bundles keep her busy and inspired.

LaVergne, TN USA
12 October 2009
160483LV00001BA